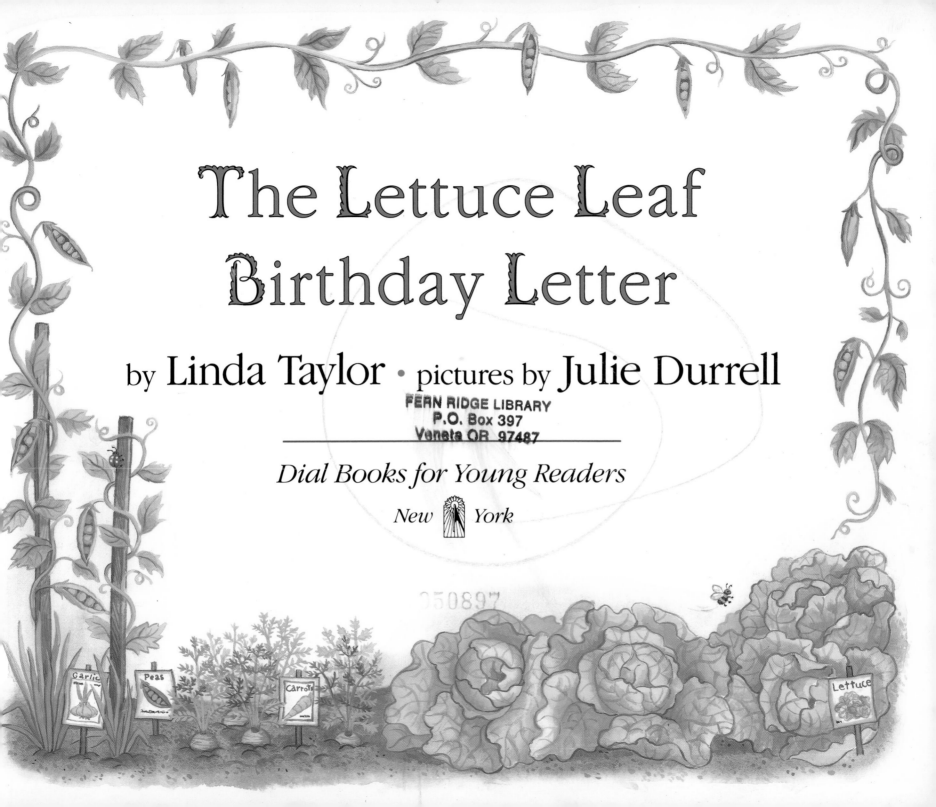

The Lettuce Leaf Birthday Letter

by Linda Taylor · pictures by Julie Durrell

Dial Books for Young Readers

New York

For Dana and Edith, in celebration of beginnings,
for Ruth in honor of endings,
and for Patrick who stood in the middle—bravely—
with both precious points in full view
L.T.

For my friend Dougie Weiss
J.D.

Published by Dial Books for Young Readers
A Division of Penguin Books USA Inc.
375 Hudson Street / New York, New York 10014

Text copyright © 1995 by Linda Taylor / Pictures copyright © 1995 by Julie Durrell
All rights reserved / First Edition
Printed in Hong Kong
1 3 5 7 9 10 8 6 4 2

Library of Congress Cataloging in Publication Data
Taylor, Linda, 1943–   The lettuce leaf birthday letter /
by Linda Taylor ; pictures by Julie Durrell.
—1st ed.   p.   cm.
Summary: A forgetful mailrabbit tries to deliver
a birthday greeting to several wrong animals before he finds the
right one, but he seems to make his customers happy wherever he goes.
ISBN 0-8037-1454-8 (trade).—ISBN 0-8037-1455-6 (library)
[1. Birthdays—Fiction. 2. Rabbits—Fiction. 3. Animals—Fiction.
4. Postal service—Letter carriers—Fiction.]
I. Durrell, Julie, ill.   II. Title.
PZ7.T21484Le   1995   [E]—dc20   93-16906   CIP   AC

The artwork was rendered in gouache with watercolors and dyes. It was
then color-separated and reproduced in red, blue, yellow, and black halftones.

It was Goose's birthday, and her best friend, Duck, did not know how to write. But Duck could paint. I will paint a birthday picture for Goose, he thought, on a big, crisp leaf of lettuce.

First he mixed the pots of paint. Red for cherries—Goose loved cherries. Yellow for tulips—Goose's favorite flower. Blue for the pond—Goose was very fond of swimming. And lots of pink—all kinds of pink. Pink for the candles. Pink for the cake. Pink for the ribbons. Goose loved pink!

Duck worked hard to get the picture just right. He was careful not to make drips and smudges...at least, not on the painting.

When the mailrabbit arrived, Duck said, "Please take this to Goose just as fast as you can. Don't forget—it's for Goose and it's very important."

Rabbit hadn't gone far when he thought, uh-oh, now who is this for? I know it's not for me. Oh, dear...

While Rabbit tried to remember who the letter was for, Goose wondered how Duck would surprise her this year.

Last year he'd sung a birthday song, and brought a big bowl of cherries. What a fine day it was!

When Rabbit crossed the bridge to Beaver's house, he found him sick in bed with a toothache.

"Ennee–mayow–faw–me?"asked Beaver. Rabbit peeked into his mail sack. One envelope had no writing on it. Maybe it's a Get Well card for Beaver, thought Rabbit.

Beaver pressed the lettuce leaf to his cheek. How cool and soothing it was.

But he could see that this was a birthday card and it wasn't his birthday.

"Dair–musht–be–shum–mishtake," said Beaver. "Dish–cawd–ish–not–faw–me."

"Hmmm," said Rabbit, putting it back in his sack. How he wished he had something for Beaver—something to make him feel better. A babbling creek ran right through Beaver's house. Rabbit stuck his paw in and loosened a puff of sweet-smelling moss from the top of an icy cold stone.

He laid it gently on Beaver's swollen cheek.

"Oh, thank you," sighed Beaver, closing his eyes. Then he drifted
off to sleep as the moss calmed the throbbing ache in his tooth.

Rabbit felt better as he continued down the road, but he still could not remember who the letter was for. Then he heard Pig tapping her hooves on her empty tin mailbox. Maybe it's for Pig!

"You're late today," Pig grumbled. "Did you bring me a letter from Hog? I hope so! He called me fat! I'm expecting a note telling me he's sorry."

Rabbit peeked into his mail sack. One envelope had no writing on it. I bet it's from Hog, thought Rabbit.

Not wasting a moment, Pig nibbled it open. "What's this?" she grunted. "There must be some mistake. It's not my birthday. This card is not for me."

"Hmmm," said Rabbit, putting it back in his sack. "What about those radishes tied to the fence?" he asked. "Are *they* for you?"

Rushing over to fetch them, Pig squealed in delight. And off she trotted, clutching the bobbing bouquet to her heart.

It was lunchtime by now, but Goose wasn't hungry. She wondered
if Duck had forgotten her birthday. Goose didn't know that right
at that moment Duck was still scrubbing paint from his feathers
and feet.

Meanwhile Rabbit made his way down the road, trying hard to remember who the envelope with no writing on it was for.

Along the way he met Owl, who had lost his glasses.

"Any mail for me?" asked Owl, squinting.

Rabbit peeked into his mail sack. One envelope had no writing on it. This is probably from someone who found Owl's glasses and is sending them back, thought Rabbit.

Owl squeezed the envelope hopefully. Then he opened it up. "Just my luck," he muttered. "There's nothing inside but a blurry, pink picture of a cake...and...candles...and who knows what else.... Even with my poor eyesight I can see that this is a birthday card. There must be some mistake. It's not my birthday. This card is not for me. Oh, I'll never find my glasses!"

"What about the glasses on top of your head?" asked Rabbit.
Owl was thrilled. "I never thought of looking there!" he hooted.

Rabbit shuffled off. It was getting late and the lettuce leaf was growing limp.

Rumpled and weary, Rabbit finally arrived at Goose's cottage. But where was Goose? She was inside—crying. "Dear, dear, Goose," said Rabbit. "What's wrong?"

"It's my birthday," sobbed Goose, "and my best friend, Duck, didn't even remember! No chocolates! No cherries! No phone call! No visit! No song at my window like last year. No NOTHING!"

"Not true!" exclaimed Rabbit. "Duck didn't forget your birthday! He gave me something to give to you. He *said* it was important. He *said* to bring it quickly. I just couldn't remember who it was for!"

Rabbit handed Goose the envelope with no writing on it.
"For you...from Duck," he said solemnly.

Goose leaped up, clucking with joy, and flapped open the envelope.

"Oh, it's beautiful! Beeeuuuutiful! Purrfect!!!" she sang.

"It was crisper this morning," said Rabbit.

Goose wasn't listening.

"Duck painted all the things I love....Cherries! Tulips!"

"I should have brought it sooner," said Rabbit. "Beaver rubbed it on his cheek."

"...And look! He drew a pond, and a big yellow sun...and a picture of me in my funny straw hat!"

"Oh, there's practically nothing left of it," cried Rabbit. "Pig nibbled off the corner by mistake!"

"...Duck remembered that pink is my very favorite color!
How thoughtful! How lovely! How splendid! How grand!"
"But Owl squeezed it!" cried Rabbit. "It's soggy! Half gone!"

"No, it's perfect," smiled Goose. "It's from my very best friend. He made it himself! He made it for me! It may be wilted, but I'll treasure it forever. Thank you for bringing it, Rabbit!"

And with that she gave Rabbit a kiss on the nose.

"Happy Birthday, dear Goose," said Rabbit, blushing. Then he hopped away with a lopsided grin, eager to get home before dark.

(He was halfway there when he realized his mail sack
was missing. But he couldn't remember where he'd left it....
Maybe at Skunk's house?)